Evil Little Things

A collection of two novelettes

Evil Little Things

A collection of two novelettes

Yasmin Bakhtiari

Gilded Dragonfly Books

ISBN: 978-1-943095-37-7 print edition

Cover Design:	Nancy Knight/GDB
Photo credit:	Depositphoto
Interior Design:	Melba Moon
Editor:	Mary Marvella/Nancy Knight

Blood for Gold
Formerly titled
Patrick O'Malley

Yasmin Bakhtiari

The entire Halloween mess started the day the terrible fog descended on Spirit Lake. The fog had lasted all day and into the night. Thick and laborious, it confused the curious townsfolk, who couldn't discern a thing through the heavy mist. When the fog finally dissipated it had produced a fresh pirate ship, like a stork leaving a new born baby in its wake. Before the fog it wasn't there, but after the fog it was. That same day Patrick O'Malley appeared on Jessica's front porch and her nightmare started.

The night before had started peacefully enough. Jessica had seen the fog over the lake from her back porch but had thought nothing of it at the time. She'd gone through her usual routine with the kids—dinner, dishes, and bedtime. Jessica missed Bryan, but he was in Ireland on a business trip and he'd told her he would be difficult to reach.

She was winding the evening down now, sitting

propped against the headboard of the bed, reading Daniel his favorite book, *Barnaby, Anna and The Witch*. Reading the Halloween fairytale, of all things, was extra special for Daniel, with Halloween lurking around the corner.

Jessica neared the end, a good thing because tonight she was extremely tired. Her eyes felt gritty and dry. She needed some good soothing eye drops, a cup of hot tea, a heating pad, a good book, and Bryan to rub her neck. But that wouldn't happen. She was too tired and lazy to make the tea, and Bryan wasn't here. She'd have to settle for eye drops and a glass of water or maybe even an ice cold beer. She shook off a mental shrug and read on.

" . . . Down below, the town's children stare up in wonder as lightning flashes and the sky booms with thunder. They all know the stories. They've all heard the rumors of Ogrish the witch and her fearsome, dark humor.

So none dare to tarry, to dawdle, or linger, afraid to be grabbed by a witch's cold fingers.

They all hurry off, against the night's coldest chill, afraid to dally and gaze at the house on the hill."

"I love Halloween," Daniel said when Jessica had finished and firmly closed the book. "It's my favorite holiday."

Jessica smiled fondly at her son. Daniel had two missing front teeth, and he was absolutely adorable. Why couldn't they stay this cute forever? With a thirteen-year-old daughter in the next room, Jessica had no illusions that her precious boy would stay precious. In a few short years he would be sawing away at the umbilical cord to get away from her, like a rat gnawing at a rope. But for now. . .

"I like Halloween, too," she told him gently. "But it's time for sleep."

"Remember, you have to check the closets, under the bed and in the bathroom and leave the closet light on."

"I remember, don't worry. But don't you think you are getting a too old for all this? You know there are no monsters."

"I know, Mommy, but just for tonight, okay?"

Daniel said that every night, but Jessica couldn't bring herself to take a firmer stand. After all, when she was a little girl she had been afraid of monsters, too.

"Okay, my darling, just for tonight."

"Can you all keep it down? I'm trying to study," Kaitlyn yelled from her room through the closed door.

Daniel rolled his eyes dramatically. "She *says* she's trying to study, but she's really on Facebook and listening to music."

"Well, maybe tonight she is really studying." Jessica ruffled his hair and kissed his cheek. "Either way, it's time for you to go to sleep."

"Okay, good night." Daniel's thumb popped into his mouth like a cork.

"Good night, sweetie, and remember that your sister is next door and I am right across the hall. Dream of kittens tonight, okay?"

The thumb cork popped out again. "I might dream of Ogrish the witch catching me with her cold fingers," Daniel said, looking at her with worried eyes.

"They learn to manipulate so young," Jessica muttered under her breath. "Then that's the last we'll be reading from that book. I'll just take it with me to my room."

The words worked like magic.

"No, that's okay, I'm not scared, good night!" And Daniel turned onto his side, away from her, and closed his eyes.

"I should have started with that," Jessica mumbled. He sure loved that book. These nightly sessions of getting Daniel off to bed were becoming more and more taxing. Things would be better when Bryan returned home. She took a deep breath. They would just start the process half an hour earlier from now on. She needed Daniel to go to bed at a decent hour so she could work on her writing.

Jessica thought of the two stories she'd been outlining, wonderingly idly if a tendency toward morbidity ran in her family. The ideas were quite grim, but she was writing it for a Halloween collection, so grim, in this case, was good. Her editor liked all her ideas so far, especially the latest ones. Her deadline was in just a few days, so she would be working much of the time, but she'd have to make sure Kaitlyn and Daniel wouldn't see what she was working on. Though Kaitlyn was five years older than Daniel, at twelve she was still a vulnerable child.

Jessica crossed the dark den to the kitchen, on the other side of the house. She grabbed a cold beer, pointedly ignored the chocolate chip cookies waiting on the table, and took a sip as she passed back through the den. She glanced at her enormous fireplace, thinking how sinister it looked in the dark and how much more pleasant it was with the lights on. She had been thinking that more and more lately, since she'd first heard several creepy rumors.

She pushed the unpleasant thoughts aside, went to her room and sat down to work on her story in the quiet, peaceful house. She flirted with ideas for her

Halloween story, struggling between an eerie leprechaun searching for a pot of gold in the bowels of a fireplace in an old Victorian home while terrorizing the family who lived there, and a woman who was so miserable in her existence that she was planning her death and funeral like a wedding. If she went with the second story it would be called "The Deading".

The leprechaun story might be a little 'too close to home' for her comfort. Rumors of the Irish who had once lived in this part of town and gossip that a pot of gold was hidden somewhere deep inside the vast fireplace of her home had given her the idea. The house had sat vacant for a while before she and Bryan bought it. It had changed owners more frequently than the other houses in the area of Spirit Lake. She hadn't heard the tales about leprechauns coming back to reclaim their pot of gold every Halloween until recently.

When she and Bryan had bought the house last December around Christmas she'd had been so excited. This would be their first Halloween in their new home. The disturbing rumors about leprechauns gave her mixed feelings. She hated to think of her lovely old Victorian home as being h*aunted*, so she decided not to add fuel to the fire by writing a fictional story about it. Maybe she would write the leprechaun story next year, after they had spent at least one Halloween here. She finally decided to write "The Deading".

***

In the very social and festive township of Spirit Lake everyone got in the spirit for holidays and special occasions. Halloween was no different. The day kept calling her, and finally Jessica decided to answer. Besides, the fog had made her curious. She had never

9

seen such dense fog before that night. The harbor of Spirit Lake had practically disappeared from view, even from her back porch. *Spooky!*

When she walked out the front door she saw that someone had left three pumpkins on the stairs to her front door. Yesterday there had been three large pumpkins. She had left them there herself, but today those three had been replaced by three much smaller pumpkins. Jessica thought this was so funny that she laughed out loud. Someone was having fun with her.

She headed toward town, where the quaint little shops were located. She would have a better view of the lake from the center of town. Maybe she would pick up a few pastries or some fresh bread from Cakes and Bakes Bakery. She passed the little park on the corner and walked the few blocks, enjoying the beautiful fall day.

Jessica had not let the fact that the house had known several different owners over the years bother her. She had been intrigued by its Victorian stature. While others might think the vastness and oldness of it would dampen the charm of the house, Jessica found the opposite to be true. When she first set eyes on the giant fireplace in the den she'd been a little taken aback. It was so big that it was obvious it was the center of the original home and over the years this old Victorian had been built around it.

Hearth and home. She smiled while she continued her walk.

When Jessica approached the heart of the small town, passed by the market and the quaint shops, and neared the dock of the bay, she couldn't help noticing what everyone else was looking at. A ship, of all things, like a pirate ship, sat right smack dab in the harbor of

Spirit Lake.

"What on earth?" Jessica began as she slowed down.

A small crowd had gathered and people spoke in hushed tones, almost like they were talking at a funeral. Jessica watched them, wondering if they even realized they were whispering. *Almost like they are afraid of waking the dead.* She shuddered.

The ship, almost pristine looking, seemed to cast a pall over the town in complete contrast to the beautiful October day. It wasn't a huge ship. The length was about sixty feet or so, and it had unusual etchings carved into the sides. In addition to a few animal carvings, some of the etchings looked Gaelic. This ship surely had Irish origins, but she kept this to herself. Small town gossip tended to spread like wildfire, and by the end of the day Jessica would have been the one who brought the ship and landed it in the harbor, just because she had said the carvings look like Gaelic Irish.

The fact that the ship looked so untouched made it look spooky. The ship, in its seeming perfection, almost *dared* onlookers to come aboard. But who knew what would be inside?

The townsfolk looked on, dour-faced but unable to look away, the way a crowd gathered around a car accident with fatal injuries. The inevitable conversation, questions, and gossip started in whispers. "Does anyone know where it came from?" someone asked.

"I'll bet it's haunted," someone else commented, and then the dam broke. Suddenly everyone was chattering, adding their two cents worth and interrupting each other. Jessica didn't even have to look around to know who was saying what. That was the thing with small towns, they could be *sooo* predictable. It was a gift and a curse.

"Maybe the town brought it in for Halloween. It certainly looks like a haunted ship."

"Maybe, but I'm not going anywhere near it," Jessica added, jumping right in.

"It looks clean and safe enough."

"Hah! It might be infested with rats."

"It might be infested with zombies."

"I say blow the damn thing up and be done with it."

"Maybe there's a pile of pirate gold hidden on the ship. The sheriff should make sure before he blows it up. Look, here comes Sheriff Martinez now."

"Who said anything about blowing up that ship?" the sheriff demanded.

His deputy, Susan Rowan, a good friend of Jessica's, stood behind him. Petite, blonde and feisty, she calmly surveyed the scene in silence.

"Don't you all start your funny talk about blowing up ships, and pirate's gold, and zombies and what not," Sheriff Martinez warned.

"You hear that? I heard something! There's something on that ship," a man called out.

Jessica had heard it, too, a noise like buzzing or a hundred dead zombies coming to life for Halloween. Or even worse, a horde of Irish leprechauns had landed to invade her house and reclaim their pot of gold.

The buzzing seemed to grow louder and the boat swayed, as if rocked by invisible hands.

The crowd gasped.

Someone actually screamed.

"That's enough!" Sheriff Martinez roared. "You folks go on now, and I don't want to see anyone around this ship 'til I figure out what's going on."

The crowd drifted away, leaving the sheriff, the deputy, the mayor and two other leading citizens of Spirit Lake deep in discussion. Jessica knew there would be no stopping folks from sniffing around that ship. She still didn't know if the ship appearing out of nowhere was a Halloween prank, but considering the attitude of the people around her, if it was a prank it was an unwelcome one.

***

Later that afternoon Jessica parked her car in the garage and took groceries into the house through the kitchen door. The kids had come in and out of the house all day through the open garage, so when Jessica noticed the smiling leprechaun standing on her front porch near the front door, her heartbeat faltered. Her first instinct was to give it good swift kick and send it flying off the porch into a neighbor's yard or into the street to let it get run over by a car. Then she composed herself. What was she thinking? It could be a neighbor's prank, maybe even the same neighbor who had switched the pumpkins on her doorstep. Or maybe the kids knew something about it.

Why had she reacted that way? It was just a silly leprechaun doll. Never mind that for her entire life she'd had an horrific aversion to dolls, especially Halloween leprechauns.

"Get a hold of yourself," she said firmly, because a mom couldn't act like a child since she had children of her own. That was an unfortunate fact of life.

She remembered the day she'd had to kill a cockroach by herself for the first time. It was one of the big brownish ones with wings, the crunchy kind. When

Kaitlyn had screamed Jessica had thought someone was trying to murder her. She'd run into her daughter's room, ready to pounce and fight and protect her young. Instead, she'd faced a horror of a different kind. And when Kaitlyn had pointed and cried, Jessica had wanted to hide and point at it, too. Since Bryan wasn't home Jessica had been forced to put on a brave face, get the bug spray, a roll of paper towels and catch the cockroach. She had killed the damn thing, but it hadn't been easy.

She'd screamed when it flew towards her, then cried when she stepped on it and it made that crunching sound. She had to wipe it up, bits of wings, roach legs and all. Her mouth had filled with hot saliva and she wanted to vomit through her tears. Kaitlyn had actually laughed at her mother's antics and still teased her to this day. Jessica had been traumatized for over a week.

She hadn't liked dolls since she was little and had watched an episode of *Twilight Zone* about an evil doll that couldn't be destroyed or gotten rid of. The damn thing kept coming back.

Ah, well, she wasn't five years old anymore, and this doll was a silly prank to remind her that a hoard of leprechauns would invade her fireplace come Halloween and search for a hidden pot of gold. If she showed her unease, not only would Kaitlyn never let her hear the end of it, but the children might pick up on her cues and be afraid, too. Jessica didn't want that. At least it wasn't a cockroach.

"Come on then, you," she told the grinning leprechaun. She picked it up and took it inside, wondering if this was like inviting a vampire into her home. Well, if so, she'd just made the biggest mistake of her life. Cockroaches, vampires and leprechauns, Halloween was around the corner, indeed.

Jessica carried the leprechaun into the kitchen and set it on the counter. She told herself she was an adult and this was just a doll, a stupid, unexpected lump of plastic. The leprechaun was big for a doll, around two and a half feet high, and looked typical for one of its breed with green clothes, buckles on the shoes, red hair and beard, and a green hat with a black band and a gold buckle. But there was something *off* about this particular leprechaun. The head was disproportionately large for its body. And she didn't care for his grin, not a good-natured, country, backslapping, corn-on-the-cob grin, but a sly, crafty grin.

Leprechauns were supposed to be mischievous by nature. Leprechauns had never interested her one way or the other. They belonged on the shelf with the other things she didn't care for. As far as she knew they were supposed to be untrustworthy. *You just can't trust a sneaky leprechaun.* And this one had a mischievous look about him.

The longer Jessica stared at it, the more engrossed she became. When she stared into its eyes she could see deepness there. As Jessica stared, a feeling of wellbeing slowly came over her. The little fellow had such a merry face she didn't know why she'd had such a bad initial reaction to him. His eyes were a twinkling blue and his rosy cheeks bloomed with hearty friendliness. Jessica hadn't noticed at first, but there was a small wind up mechanism in its back. She decided not to wind it up. The thought of it made her feel uncomfortable, almost like opening Pandora's Box.

Jessica looked back at its face. It seemed to

have changed. Now the blue eyes held a knowing look and the smile was wise and as old as the hills. Jessica frowned. There was something in that smile. An odd feeling washed over her again, and this time she could swear she smelled the green fresh scent she associated with Ireland, though she had never been there. That's where Bryan was now. Bryan Fitzgerald-the name was pure Irish. The feeling swept over her again, and she put her doubts aside and smiled back at the doll.

As she did, something akin to the sound of bagpipes began playing in her mind. The pleasant sound made her feel content. Jessica pushed him out of the way next to some potted plants and started dinner. Then she went into the den and phoned Bryan, but he didn't answer.

When the kids sat down for supper Jessica quizzed them.

"I didn't bring the leprechaun home," Kaitlyn said. "I don't know where he came from."

"Me, neither," piped Daniel. "Maybe we should hide the Lucky Charms."

When Kaitlyn actually laughed at Daniel's joke Jessica smiled at the two of them.

"Can I keep him in my room?" Daniel asked.

"*No!*" Jessica wanted to shout but stopped herself in time. But the kids must have seen something in her expression, something she wasn't even aware of herself.

Daniel, suddenly deflated, said abruptly, "Never mind, I don't want him."

Jessica was at a loss for words. To her relief, Kaitlyn offered to get him ready for bed and read to him. Thank goodness for small favors.

***

Fire, light, the dawn of thinking man and civilization. Heat, the very core of every hearth and home. Tonight she stood in front of the bleak and desolate fireplace. Nothing about it seemed cheerful or welcoming at the moment. The empty hearth seemed so stark, black, menacing and so. . . deep.

She remembered making love with Bryan in front of this very fireplace, warmed by cheery flames. He'd heard the stories about the hidden pot of gold inside the fireplace and would tease her, beating his bare chest and chanting his favorite Irish phrase in a low voice so as not to wake the kids, *"Erin go Braugh!"* which meant 'Ireland forever'. He'd joke that he was named after Bryan Boru, the Lion of Ireland, once the High King of the Irish. Then they'd make slow, delicious love in front of the crackling flames, and he would murmur sweet nothings into her ear.

"*Mo cuishle . . . mo cuishle, mo cuishle*, my love, my darling, my blood. *Chuisle mo chroí,* pulse of my heart. . ."

A sudden wind whistled through the house. A high keening wail from the fireplace made Jessica jump. She swallowed a gasp. It was almost as if the fireplace had read her mind. Although she knew she was being silly, she shivered. There was no cheery fire crackling away. In the evening hours it was easy to believe that a hoard of evil leprechauns would make their way into her life, into her home to reclaim their pot of gold and lay waste to anyone who got in their way.

Jessica thought of the doll she had dubbed Patrick O'Malley. She looked over her shoulder into the kitchen, where she had left it. For a moment she was so taken aback that the hair stood up on the back of her neck. Though the doll was where she had left it, right in her line of vision, for a moment it looked like his head was cocked and he actually peered at her from the kitchen. His dancing blue eyes and ruddy good humor mocked her. Jessica frowned. She knew she was being silly, but she hadn't left the doll there in a pose that would let him see into the den.

"Stop it now," she told herself loudly. Her voice, spoken aloud and to no one in the solitary room, scared her even more.

Obviously Kaitlyn or Daniel had moved the thing when they were helping her clean up. That's all there was to it. She had a good mind to open the kitchen door and pitch the doll right out the back door.

But Jessica knew the truth. And the truth was that she really didn't want to go near it. She thought of the *Twilight Zone* episode "Living Doll", the one where the doll kept coming back, creeping and stealthy, soft-footed on silent doll feet. Jessica had hated that episode, but at the same time had always been intrigued by it. And now, like an episode of the *Twilight Zone* come true, the hour grew late. She thought of lying in her bed, going to sleep with nothing illuminating the room but the light of the glowing moon through the bedroom window. She would suddenly see the outline of Patrick O'Malley's head as he tried to find a way back in, perhaps tapping ever so softly on the window pane, tap, tap-tap, tap-tap-tap. . .

If she saw something like that she would let out a bloodcurdling scream so horrifying it would wake the dead. And she thought that if she put the doll out, even if she drove with it in the car and threw it out on some isolated farm or in a dumpster with a heavy, metal lid, that Patrick O'Malley might just visit her in the wee hours of the night.

It was all ridiculous, but right now in the dark anything could happen, anything was believable. The most outlandish and sinister seeds of the mind took root and burgeoned in the dark. Phantoms grew wings, fireplaces had secret passages, husbands were the descendants of dead kings, and evil leprechauns lay in wait, lurking in the shadows, whispering and waiting to reclaim lost treasures of gold.

Jessica wasn't interrupted by anything but her dreams that night. In her dream she danced around the dark fireplace. The opening gaped like mouth, a charred and black yawning pit from hell. And the fireplace had eyes in that deep chasm of a pit, and they watched her dance a jig in a long, old fashioned skirt, and she had buckles on her shoes. Then she cried out, *"Erin go Braugh!"* and jumped into the fireplace, falling down, down, down into waiting hands, her death the key to unlocking the hidden treasure, while Patrick O'Malley wildly played a fiddle and laughed.

In the morning the wisps of Jessica's dream had faded to a fuzzy blur and only tickled the dark recesses of her mind, like little demonic thieves waiting for her to sleep so they could come out to play.

***

Jessica had no trouble achieving a dark tone when she sat down to work on her story, "The Deading." Although the tale was grim, she had injected a slight hint of macabre humor.

It was fiendishly bizarre and quite clever. When she stopped for the morning, Jessica found the results both surprising and pleasing. Pleasing, because it was coming along better than she had expected, and surprising, because it was quite grim. She approved.

She read back over the first few pages.

Jessica sighed with satisfaction. She thought about the night before and realized she might even owe the stupid leprechaun a bit of thanks for putting her in such a weird mood. She decided to stop for a short break. She would let the children have pizza tonight, because she was on a deadline and she needed to have this story completed within the next two days.

Jessica opened the front door to go for a walk. The morning was colder than usual for this time of year, but she found the nippy air exhilarating. When she came home she took a nice, hot shower then worked on her story for another hour.

She stopped and strolled into the kitchen. At this pace she would be finished by tomorrow afternoon, at the latest. Lost in thought about her story and how much she missed Bryan, she put some water in a kettle to boil and thought about dinner. Maybe she wouldn't have to order pizza, after all, but she had already promised. She would compensate and ease her guilty conscience by making a salad.

She looked in the refrigerator and got started. After she put the finishing touches on the salad she would start a load of laundry. She was reaching for the salt and pepper when she saw Patrick O'Malley back beside the potted plants near the sink. He was no longer at the edge of the counter, peering into the living room. One of the kids had probably pushed the doll away from the edge of the counter.

In spite of herself Jessica found herself drawn to the leprechaun.

When she picked it up a feeling of contentment flowed through her again. In her mind's eye she saw green valleys. She imagined eating boiled potatoes dipped in salt, and she could hear the sound of bagpipes playing throughout rolling green hills filled with heather. The feeling almost overpowered her. She caressed the doll almost lovingly and felt the wind up mechanism in its back. No one was home. It wouldn't hurt to wind it up. Perhaps it played music. Perhaps...

Jessica wound up the dial. Then she let it go and set it on the counter. She waited intently, and then she heard something, a rhythmic sound, the beat of dancing music. The sound captivated her, and before she knew it she closed her eyes and took it all in. Little by little Jessica drifted, floating on magical wings to another time and place, a place with rainbows and the scents of heather, and mists rising atop lochs of the pure, crystal water. And then she heard spirited music, the likes of which she'd never heard before.

Patrick O'Malley's spindly green legs seemed to come alive and kick and jive in time to the music. His large head seemed to nod in time to the beat. Jessica laughed out loud in spite of herself. She found herself clapping in time to the rhythm. Her feet picked up the beat and started tapping in a rhythmic tattoo. Then suddenly she was dancing along with the lively music, the buckles on her shiny black shoes flashing in the light as she swished about in her long green skirts. She was young and tireless, and suddenly Bryan was there dancing with her, kissing her laughing mouth, leaving her breathless with excitement. And then he spun her about, around and around and around. Nothing mattered except the dance, nothing mattered except being young and happy. Nothing mattered except...

The gold.

Aye, my bonnie lass, there's a good girl. Just a little closer. We need you to join us. You are the key. Mo cuishla, my darling, my blood. Mo cuishle...

Was that Bryan's voice? He had run off, but he called her now to join him, and she had to find him. Maybe he was there, behind the thick copse of alder trees. She made her way to the dense brushes and pushed the branches aside.

"Mom!" Kaitlyn's cry stunned Jessica back into the present.

"What's going on, what are you doing? Why are you standing there?"

Jessica blinked. The music had stopped. The fresh green smells of Ireland had vanished, as well, and the delicious smells of boiled potatoes dipped in butter and salt. And Bryan was gone, too.

"What?" Jessica murmured. "Nothing. Nothing is going on."

Kaitlyn and Daniel stood near the kitchen, watching her as if she was some kind of monster. Where was she? She turned around and realized she perched on the fireplace hearth, moving the screen to the side. She suddenly felt dizzy.

"Mommy, what were you doing?" Daniel asked. He looked ready to cry.

Jessica thought quickly. "Nothing. I mean, I was thinking about starting a fire tonight. It was so cold today. I wanted to surprise you. I'm almost finished with the story and I thought we would celebrate with dinner in here in front of the fire." Instantly Jessica experienced a dark feeling, blackness, desolation, and smoldering anger. This was coming from the doll. Jessica understood now. She understood everything.

"Really?" Kaitlyn looked doubtful, but Daniel looked excited.

"Yes," Jessica answered. "Pizza and a movie in

front of a nice fire on a cold October night. And salad. Of course you have to do your homework first."

She shooed them off before they could complain or whine. They were now telling her what kind of pizza they wanted. Jessica sat on the sofa and sighed in relief. She had just scraped by. If Daniel and Kaitlyn hadn't stopped her, she'd have unlatched the protective seal of the fireplace, moved the heavy grate and jumped inside, falling to her death. The whole thing had been some kind of trick. She would probably have thought she was diving into a beautiful loch, but really she would have been plummeting to her demise and into the waiting hands of the leprechauns, who had probably been brought over on that ship. Was it really a coincidence that at this very moment Bryan was in Ireland, of all places?

She understood now. She, Jessica Fitzgerald, had to be the one to unlock some curse and free the pot of gold. She didn't know the reason, and she didn't care. Maybe Bryan was truly some Irish King, and she was the sacrificial wife. She could give a rat's behind about some wicked pot of gold. They could have it, but she wouldn't let herself be killed by falling into a dark fire pit, into the catacombs and crypts of Irish lore.

The whole thing sounded ridiculous, and she might be crazy, and yet she knew she wasn't. She wasn't afraid anymore. She was mad. Her eyes narrowed. She planned to start the biggest fire she could. After that she would throw the damn leprechaun straight to Hades in a fiery blaze of glory.

Jessica started the fire in the fireplace, as planned. It wasn't easy. It took tremendous determination to open the safety latch on the floor of the fireplace. The pit of darkness went very deep. If she had been still brainwashed, it would have been easier. She would have thought she was picking flowers or something. But suddenly she managed to move the heavy iron grate about one foot. She couldn't do more than that. But there was just enough of a space for one evil little leprechaun to go hurtling down into the bowels of Irish hell.

When the pizza arrived the kids helped their plates and watched the movie. Jessica played along, but her mind wandered elsewhere. Maybe she should catch the leprechaun up in a pillow case. Or maybe she would just go and get him and throw him down the fire pit. When the kids had gone into their rooms, Jessica went and stoked up the fire. She pushed the logs to the side, leaving that small space open that she would throw the doll into. Then she went into the kitchen.

She looked everywhere to no avail.

Patrick O'Malley had disappeared.

***

Halloween had finally arrived. The ship was still docked in the harbor. Jessica could see it from her deck, but she hadn't gone back into town. Susan Rowan had told Jessica that she and Sheriff Martinez, the mayor, and Old Luke Fletcher had finally gone aboard the ship. They had found a gold piece and a lock of hair on the desk. Jessica asked, though she had known that the hair would be red. They also found an old belt with a metal clasp with ancient inscriptions carved into it. Jessica knew again this would be Gaelic, but she didn't comment.

Now Jessica, alone in the house, worked on the ending of her story. Kaitlyn and Daniel had gone trick-or-treating with Susan Rowan and her family. She worked on her computer in her room. Outside it had started to rain hard. Jessica felt a little uneasy alone in her house with her morbid story. Should she be frightened? She wondered what had happened to Patrick O'Malley, but quickly put him out of her mind. She couldn't dwell on his disappearance. She couldn't rationalize the unexplainable because it was impossible. She would only succeed in frightening herself. Instead, she concentrated on finishing her story. She wrote on, finally coming to the end.

A perfect ending. She wrote the last two words and sat back. Done, Jessica saved a copy and sent it to her editor, Nancy. It seemed important that she send it right away. The rain sounded even harder, if that was possible, and a boom of thunder cracked loudly through the night's sky. Jessica shivered. Then suddenly the lights went out. Jessica screamed.

Her harsh breathing was the only sound in the darkness. Jessica felt along the wall as she crept down the dark hallway. She felt something watching her from the darkness, a creature from her earliest childhood nightmares. A monster crouched and waited in the closet at night, ready to pounce and gobble her up. Or a scaly creature lurked under her bed, with reptilian yellow eyes and sharp teeth, waiting for her to put her feet on the floor before it reached out and clasped its slimy hand around her ankle.

These thoughts of something watching her, hiding in her house, waiting in stealth and silence, threatened to paralyze Jessica. She wanted to squeeze her eyes shut and pretend none of this was happening.

But all this was nonsense, because Jessica had an idea of what waited for her and knew she had to be strong. She should have known it would happen when she was by herself. She could hear it now. Quiet, furtive sounds moving softly with whisper quiet in the darkness, assuring her she wasn't alone. Was she imagining that soft tread creeping through her house in the dark? Had her mind conjured up the almost imperceptible sound of the drawer in the kitchen slowly sliding open ever so gently, something or someone easing out her sharpest and most lethal knife? A cold prickle of goose bumps broke out on the back of her neck and down her arms.

As she tiptoed toward the kitchen Jessica stumbled into her baseball bat leaning against the wall and squelched an ear piercing scream. Once she realized it was only her baseball bat she grabbed it, thankful for the weapon. Right now she had enough adrenaline pumping through her veins to decapitate a vampire or, at the very least, an evil, little leprechaun.

Jessica readied her bat. She had made her way to the kitchen. The rain pelted against the window, muffling the sound of her harsh breathing. In the darkness of the kitchen she saw a shadow of something on the counter. With the moon's light shining through the window, she could see the outline of Patrick O'Malley's evil, mischievous head. At the same time, from behind her Jessica heard another low, keening wail, like a deathly howl, come from the fireplace. A gust of cold swept through the house. Jessica whimpered. Were they coming through the fireplace?

A bolt of lightning rent the sky. An ear splitting crack of thunder ripped through the house. This time Jessica screamed loudly. She heard the sounds of someone trying to open the door. She imagined a horde of leprechauns scrambling against the door and muttering gibberish, coming to meet their leader, Patrick O'Malley. With their strong hairy hands they would carry her through the den and into the fireplace. They would have no trouble pushing the heavy iron grating away from the floor of the fireplace. They would push her inside to fall to her doom in the thick, fetid darkness, unlocking the curse of the pot of gold.

But when the front door flew open Kaitlyn and Daniel stood with Susan Rowan. Jessica had been silly to think the evil leprechauns would come through the front door like guests. "What happened?" Susan asked, rushing to Jessica's side. Susan flipped the light switch. Surprisingly, or not so surprisingly, the lights came back on. "Why are you standing here in the dark? Are you okay?"

"The lights went off," Jessica answered, running her hand through her hair. "I heard a noise in the house and then sound of the thunder. I guess I just got scared." Her eyes darted to the fireplace. It was innocently quiet.

"Understandable," Susan said in her deputy voice. Then her eyes widened. "What's that?"

Jessica followed the direction of Susan's stare, and there was Patrick O'Malley, with his large head and his merry smile, standing on her counter. His blue eyes had lost their crafty gleam for the moment, staring innocently ahead into space. Jessica's heart pounded against her chest. The kitchen drawer was open. And one of her sharpest knives lay on the floor near the leprechaun. It looked as if he had been startled and dropped it.

It took Susan Rowan a long moment before she could tear her gaze away. Then she looked at Jessica closely. "What's going on here?"

For a moment Jessica wanted to tell her everything, because she knew Susan was aware of the leprechaun rumors surrounding her house, and Jessica knew she could trust Susan, but she changed her mind in an instant. Susan might try to take the doll with her, and Jessica knew there was only one place that leprechaun needed to go. She was going to stuff that thing into the fireplace. The gate was still open and ready to receive.

She composed her features carefully. "I told you I was scared. I was getting a knife for protection."

"But you already have a bat," Susan said reasonably. "Why the knife?"

"I wanted both," Jessica blurted out.

The two women stared at each other for a long moment.

"Is there something you want to tell me?" Susan asked quietly. "You know you can tell me anything. I'm here for you."

"Mom?" Kaitlyn asked.

"Go to your rooms," Jessica said a little abruptly. "Say thank you to Susan and go." She turned to Susan. "Really, it's nothing. But thank you. You saved the day. Now 'tis time ye were off to enjoy what's left of this lovely evening. Enough of this blarney."

Jessica stopped in shock. What had she just said? Had she actually said *ye* and *blarney*? What was happening to her?

Susan Rowan froze. "You just spoke with an Irish brogue," she said evenly.

Jessica's face turned red and she snatched up the leprechaun firmly. She thought she could feel a tug of it trying to get away. "I was just joking," she answered. She needed Susan to go before she started to dance an Irish jig and spew nonsense like, *my bonnie wee lass*. It was Halloween, after all, and time was running out. It was all or nothing. When Susan finally turned to go Jessica followed her to the door. She waved, not trusting herself to speak. She closed the door and didn't even go down the hall to speak to Daniel or Kaitlyn. She went straight to the fireplace. As she got closer she imagined darkness, famine, despair and anger. Patrick O'Malley was putting up a fight. Such darkness surrounded her she could barely breathe or see. A tremor of pain began to build inside her head.

But Jessica wouldn't give up easily. She shook the doll roughly. "Think y're going to slice me up with a carving knife, do you, me foin, wee man?"

She had kept the fire smoldering and the opening accessible because she had known the leprechaun would come back. With one hand she pushed the metal screen aside and pushed the doll toward the hole. The whole fireplace seemed to shudder and moan. The pain in Jessica's head grew stronger, and she could feel her hold on the leprechaun starting to slip.

An evil giggle filled her head. Patrick O'Malley was getting the upper hand, and in a moment the whole fireplace would come tumbling down around her and she would be buried alive and then go crashing down into the pit of the fireplace.

"*Erin go Braugh!*"

Jessica heard the triumphant scream, and the whole hearth seemed to quake. Jessica heard Daniel's and Kaitlyn's voices. She could hear their confusion and terror.

"Who will take care of them now?" She wondered aloud. How could she leave them in the evil hands of this devil.

Not in this lifetime. Jessica tightened her grip on

the slippery doll and quick as a wink she stuffed him down the hole. The doll seemed to scream, but whether it was in her mind or not, she couldn't tell.

"A curse on yer bones, Patrick O'Malley!" Jessica shouted and wondered again if she was losing her mind. Not only was her speech Irish-like, but now even her voice held an Irish lilt. She shuddered. She could almost feel herself shrinking down to two feet tall, with fiery red hair and wild blue eyes.

A cloud of dust and ash erupted from the bowels of the deep fireplace and rose up like putrid fumes from hell and engulfed her. She coughed and sputtered. Stone began crumbling and falling around her. One struck her on the head. The last thing she thought before darkness claimed her was that the kids, at least, were safe.

***

Jessica slowly awakened. She clawed her way up through depths of darkness, but instead of screaming with terror, she found comfort from the sound of Bryan's voice. At once she felt a calmness, almost a sense of giddiness. She fought the darker feelings down for a moment. She felt as if weights held her down, but at the same time she floated up. At length she opened her eyes. It was early evening, the beginning of dusk. And then she heard Daniel squeal with excitement, and she saw Bryan, her husband, finally returned to her.

"Bryan, you're home!" Jessica cried and threw her arms around his neck. "You're home, at last! I've missed you." She gazed at her husband, drinking in the sight of him.

"I'm home now," Bryan soothed, stroking her hair. "You gave us quite a scare, my love."

His gaze held her warmly, and suddenly Jessica felt relieved, because she was sure everything had been a dream. She had just bumped her head. She was fine now. She and the kids were safe, and Bryan was home. She basked in the comfort and love of her little family.

"How come I didn't go the hospital?" Jessica asked, frowning.

"The paramedics came. They took all your vital signs and said you were just knocked out and needed rest," Kaitlyn told her. "Then Dr. Jones came by and checked you over. She said you'd be awake soon." Then Dad came, but Deputy Rowan stayed with us until then.

Thank goodness for Susan. When did you come? How long was I out? were the questions on the tip of Jessica's tongue, the questions she meant to ask, but to her surprise she asked about the ship instead. "Ship?" Bryan asked, and Kaitlyn and Daniel looked confused.

"Yes, the mysterious ship in the harbor. Don't you remember?" she asked Kaitlyn and Daniel.

"No, Mom," Kaitlyn said. "There wasn't any ship. But your editor called. She said she sent an email and you hadn't answered. She said she loved your story."

"Really, that's great," Jessica felt better already.

"I'm home now, my bonnie lass, and I brought you a present. I know it's a little late for Halloween, but I know you like to decorate for holidays."

Bryan produced a large box. Kaitlyn and Daniel stood beside him, smiling. Jessica felt a stirring of unease ripple through her. The size of the box was about two and a half feet long. What would be in that box?

Outside, the rain grew heavier. A quake of

thunder erupted, and for a second the lights in the room flashed off and then on again. In the brief moment that the lights flashed off, and the room was only lit up by moonlight from the window, Jessica saw the three of them grinning, with wild red hair and glowing red eyes. It happened so quickly she knew she had imagined it. Bryan, perhaps, but not her own sweet children.

Her eyes filled with tears and her hands trembled.

"What's wrong, Mom?" Kaitlyn asked.

"Open it," Daniel said, grinning his toothless grin.

"Honey?" Bryan asked. "What is it?"

They all look so normal, so concerned. Jessica shook her head to clear it and took a breath. "Nothing," she said. "Nothing is wrong." She wondered what she had looked like in that moment of darkness when the thunder had boomed and the lights had flashed out for a second. None of her real questions would ever be answered. But it didn't matter, because some things were just meant to be. Sometimes the darkness just didn't make sense.

Jessica's hands trembled. They all waited for her to open her gift. She opened it. Was it a dream or just fate? She wondered when the merry leprechaun smiled up at her from inside the box. He looked good as new, but Jessica could see the tiny smudge of ash on his green sleeve.

For a secret moment shared between the two of them when everyone was busy and excited, the doll gave Jessica a hearty wink. Bryan and the kids had been talking and of course hadn't seen anything. Jessica couldn't make out what they were saying. Really, she didn't care. She could only hear one thing at the moment as the tears rolled down her face. A special voice, meant for her ears alone.

"*Erin go Braugh*! Long live Ireland! *Mo cuishle,* my darling, my blood. *Chuisle mo chroí.*"

Patrick O'Malley, her blood, pulse of her heart, had returned home.

Be Careful What You Wish For

Yasmin Bakhtiari

On the waning hours of the late spring afternoon, on the day before the Magna Con, in her little house on Elm Street Abby planned for the upcoming weekend eagerly. Tomorrow she would take her place among thousands of con goers in downtown Atlanta.

A thrill raced through her, but her movements were disjointed as if her thoughts were all askew. Though she was fretful by nature, she was determined not to let this deter her. Each year she looked forward to this event like a child anticipating Christmas, and this year would mark her most importance attendance yet.

Abby just loved the Con. It was one of the few public places where she could be herself. She could dress up and cart around her little family of broken dolls in her red wagon, arousing the suspicion of no one. But, as excited as she was about the Con, Abby was also quite anxious because her package, the one holding the key to all her wishes and dreams hadn't arrived yet, and it was imperative she get it tonight.

And, of course, she dreaded the unpleasant task of dealing with Patti.

Abby looked around at her assortment of disfigured dolls. She collected all kinds, amassed them the way lonely old ladies collected cats. They had been beautiful once, but all were now mutilated in some way—missing eyes, cracked faces and bald spots where hair had been ripped out—their ruination caused by Patti's spiteful ways.

Ah, jealous Patti, always nasty to the others, but Abby still loved her unconditionally, but at the moment, her most special doll, constant companion and best friend was nowhere to be seen. This, in itself, was not surprising. Patti always acted out whenever Abby got a new delivery. But she didn't have time to worry about Patti now. She had to get ready for tomorrow.

She tried to concentrate on packing, but time and time again she paused and glanced at the clock on her nightstand by the bed. If it got too late the delivery would be postponed.

She crossed the room and stared out into the night. The oncoming twilight soothed her. The orange ball of the sun hovering against the horizon offered tranquility, but the wind had picked up and the trees flailed like fluttering hands drumming against the blackening sky. The brewing storm cast splatters of rain against the window shattering the muted silence of her little world.

The lights flickered. Abby worried they would go out and she would be cast in darkness. So unpleasant. She only welcomed darkness on her own terms.

A soft voice crept up behind her.

"And what are you waiting for, dearest Abby?"

Abby squelched a shriek. The voice, high pitched yet softly spoken, pierced through her thoughts. Abby knew this voice as well as her own, but was still startled, for the childlike whisper was a puff of breath against the soft down of her neck, so close, and so very sly.

"Patti!" she cried, whipping around, "you scared me!" Abby kept her tone light, but her heart thumped frantically for a moment before settling down. No one was behind her.

The branches of the lashing trees scratched against the window pane. But beneath the scratching was another sound, a tapping, a grating.

"Patti? Is that you?"

Abby peered out into the rainy gloom. A keen wail thrummed around the house like the whining cry of a child. Patti's face suddenly appeared in the window, staring back at her from the glassed plane, a fragmented image of the doll's already ravaged face. Abby screamed. Patti's face melted into a mask of rage and disappeared.

She heard a rustle from her dresser, barren except for an antique music box. It creaked open softly, the sound tiny in the quiet room. Even the scratching against the window pane stopped.

Whatever had been brewing outside was inside now.

The lights flickered and went out. Abby froze. She heard the tiny clicks of the music box winding. A hushed pause filled the quiet then the sound of a melody. The macabre notes of Poe's classic poem, now set to music, "Come Little Children" played. The eerie strains filled the room, the tinkling notes ominous in the darkness.

From the shadows, Abby discerned the silhouette of the music box, the glimmer of its silver reflected in the moonlight. If she reached out she could pluck the notes from the air before they blew away like mist burning off the river. The eerie music, so hauntingly lovely, yes, so lovely . . . Abby closed her eyes, her thoughts drifted as she listened.

One, two, three, One, two, three . . .

She nodded sleepily in time to the music.

The melody twinkled darkly. All around her, Abby's room full of broken dolls began to shift and stir, as if roused from a deep slumber. Slowly they floated upwards from their perches, puppets lifted by invisible strings. Enthralled by the spectacle, Abby watched. The dolls rose higher, their little feet dangled listlessly. Their eyes stared blankly as they slowly swayed in time to a waltz.

One, two, three, one, two, three . . .

The lyrics played in Abby's head. The vacant stares were frightening in the darkened room, but Abby was trapped in silver threads of a web woven just for her and couldn't move. The music continued. She heard the Gregorian chanting of children, dolls singing from the grave.

"Come little children, I'll take thee away,
Into a land of enchantment . . .
Come little children, the time's come to play,
Here in my garden of shadows . . ."

The rising dolls hovered. Their little hands moved stiffly, reaching out to one another. They ghosted softly and slowly towards the ceiling, peering down at Abby, their sightless eyes gazing blindly in the night filled room.

The music continued, its waltz-pace slow and spellbinding.

One, two, three, one, two, three,
One, two, three, one, two, three . . .

"follow sweet children
I'll show thee the way
Through all the pain
and the Sorrows . . ."

Weep not poor children
For life is this way
Murdering beauty and passions . . ."

Abby, too, felt weightless, carried by the funereal timbre of the melody. A hand seemed to reach out and grip her heart so that it thudded slowly, pulsing in time to the music. Ah, Patti, wicked creature that she was. This was Patti's doing Abby thought groggily.

"Come out, come out, wherever you are," she called in a thick dazed voice.

"Come out, come out, wherever you are," echoed a tiny mocking voice.

In her mind's eye, Abby saw the doll hiding in the shadows, gimlet eyed and waiting, stifling a high pitched giggle behind a white porcelain hand.

"Come dance with me," Abby said drunkenly. And suddenly Patti was in Abby's arms, forgiving her, and they waltzed and swayed together in time to the music, as the world spun crazily around them.

Outside the wind moaned and rattled against the house, but inside Abby waltzed with Patti. The dolls, high above, held hands and drifted brokenly, staring down at her with their smashed faces and soulless eyes. The rhythm pulsed in her head.

"One two three, one two three . . .
Come out and play with me . . ."

"Hush now dear children,
It must be this way
To weary of life and deceptions,

Rest now my children
For soon we'll away
Into the calm and the quiet . . ."

The jarring sound of the doorbell buzzed, shattering the dark mood in the little room. The music stopped abruptly on a jangling discordant note. Abby gasped. The childish singing in her head echoed away. The music box clapped shut. The spell was broken. High above, the broken dolls hovered for a moment, suspended in time, then dropped suddenly like so many dead bodies, thumping against the floor. They lay strewn about Abby's feet like crumpled little corpses.

Abby blinked. The pounding in her heart matched the fading rhythm in her mind. She looked around. The lights were on in her room again, the shadows, gone. Abby wiped her hand across her forehead. Her dolls! She looked around. All was as it should be, except for Patti. Abby had forgotten about her for the moment.

The harsh buzz sounded a second time, but this time Abby was herself. A rush of excitement and fear coursed through her, tingling from the roots of her hair straight down to her finger tips. It was finally here! Now her dreams would come true. But behind her excitement, in the hollows and valleys of her lonely soul, she heard Patti's soft warning, *"Be careful what you wish for, dearest Abby."* before fading away.

Abby was too excited to take heed. She hurried up the steps and avoided looking at her reflection in the hall mirror she passed by it. She had contemplated at one time smashing all her bathroom mirrors and removing the decorative ones around the house but had decided against it. If someone came into her home, what would they think?

She peered out the window by the front door. Whoever had buzzed the doorbell was gone. She cracked the door open and saw a package against the base of the planter by the front door. *The doll sized box I've been waiting for.*

She carried the box to her room and placed it on her canopied bed. She held her breath as she tore away the wrapping, revealing a light colored wooden box painted with ornate flowers. Abby unlatched the metal clasp and opened the painted lid. She lifted her hands before the box, a sorceress raising her hands before a glowing crystal ball, and gasped at the treasure nestled within the folds and layers of tissue paper.

A brand new porcelain doll, a mirror image of herself, stared back up at her, only this doll had perfect flawless skin and long curling hair.

"Ooooh, you're perfect," she told the doll. If only she could look like this again, the way she used to look before the fire. How she wished she had porcelain perfect skin, smooth and unscarred, the way her dolls looked before Patti got a hold of them, the way she herself once was.

But Pattie wouldn't touch this doll, Abby would

make certain. If this doll was ruined it would defeat her whole purpose of having it custom made.

For the rest of the evening Abby was busy. Finally, satisfied that all was ready, she sighed in relief. She had her new Abby doll in her sight at all times. And she knew Patti would come out of hiding eventually.

"Magna Con, here I come," she murmured and went to sleep.

***

The Hyatt Regency Atlanta bustled with activity. Abby found herself among the hordes attending the Con. The streets and hotels were alive with the festive atmosphere. Thousands of people like her waited all year for the event, but Abby's love of the Con went beyond her attraction for science fiction.

The element of the Con itself was mysterious and far reaching. Anything could happen here. And all the costumes! Some were so elaborate they looked like they had just come from a movie set, while other attendees were more humbly adorned, clad in simple Magna Con t-shirts. Abby fit right in, pulling her little wagon of creepy dolls. Of course no one thought anything was amiss.

Dressed to match the little occupants in her red wagon, Abby had adorned a wig of long, curling ringlets and a floral, lace-hemmed dress and bravely marched through the crowds of the Con. No, not bravely, really. She'd painted her face and rouged her cheeks and wore a large sun hat so no one could detect her true hideousness. She hated the thick ropey feel of her scarred face. But things were about to change. Abby shivered with excitement. The timing was perfect. All she had to do was remember what she had learned about enchantments and dark magic and contact

Crystal, the fortune teller. Crystal always attended the Con and would know how to proceed. Then the magic of Magna Con would fulfill Abby's wishes.

She found the first workshop with no trouble since she'd been here before and settled herself at the end of a row, pushing her wagon a little out of the way, and pulled Patti onto her lap. They had made up, and to placate her Abby had adorned them in matching dresses and left her new Abby doll in her room on the bed. This delighted Patti, as Abby knew it would. Patti was quite possessive.

As her gaze swept the crowd, she noticed a young man watching her. For a moment a wave of nostalgia washed over her because he seemed so familiar, but the moderator was about to introduce the panel for the session, so Abby turned in her seat, pulling away ever so slightly from the people around her, and hugged Patti closer to her.

For the next hour she sat enthralled, loving every minute of the panel discussion before her. When it ended Abby waited for the room to empty a little so she would have more room to maneuver her wagon before she exited. She seriously contemplated taking it up to her room and leaving it there so she could travel about unencumbered.

Finding space for herself and her wagon of dolls was especially difficult and annoying to the people around her. One boisterous man in particular barked a rude comment in the elevator until Patti's head snapped around and stared at him. That had shut his mouth real fast.

The other people in the elevator had laughed, some uneasily. They obviously thought this was part of the allure of the Con, but Abby needed to have another stern talk with Patti. Even if she left her wagon in the room, she would take Patti along with her. She didn't dare anger Patti and then leave her alone in the room with the others.

"Abby?"

Abby looked up, startled out of her thoughts and equally surprised that anyone would know her. She usually kept to herself. She stared at the familiar looking handsome man in front of her.

"Abby, it's me, Jeremy, Jeremy Walker."

Abby continued staring like a zombie.

"That is you, isn't it?" Jeremy asked, smiling tentatively, suddenly looking a little uncertain.

Abby finally found her voice. Her mouth was suddenly dry. "Jeremy?"

He looked relieved. "How are you?"

"Uh, how did you recognize me?" she asked in surprise. Her mind wanted to scream, *"It's him! It's Jeremy!,"* but instead she said in a steady voice, "It's been so long." *Yes, too long. I buried you along with the ghosts of my past when I never saw you again. You disappeared when I needed you most.* But she kept these thoughts to herself.

"Are you kidding?" Jeremy said, smiling. "I'd recognize you anywhere."

Patti quivered in Abby's arms. Abby clamped her arm tight around her.

"Is something wrong?" he asked. He glanced at Abby, then at the doll she held. His eyes flickered across the ravaged features.

"Hey, is that—"

"Yes," Abby said hurriedly. "It's Patti. You remember her, don't you?"

Abby's eyes held a shuttered look, a warning?

And Jeremy knew instinctively not to mention Patti's disfigurement, the last time he had seen the doll was before the fire, before Abby had been lost to him. The doll had been okay then. She must have been messed up in the fire that burned down Abby's house.

For Abby, seeing Jeremy was a shock. She never thought she'd see him again and was grateful heavy makeup concealed her scars.

"He thinks you're ugly now, that's why he left you all alone,"

Patti's whispers haunted her memories. Could Patti have been lying? Suddenly it seemed possible.

Jeremy's kind eyes, eyes she had remembered for so long until she had made herself forget, looked warm and concerned. For a moment Abby felt lost in time, transported to those days when she had been so happy, before everything had gone to hell, and Jeremy had abandoned her like everyone else did. Or so she'd thought. But this man who stood before her, this man he'd become—this was the Jeremy she remembered, not the bogeyman she had decided he was when she never heard from him again. When Patti's sly whispers had become nightmares in her head.

"Are you okay?"

She realized she had been lost in thought and Jeremy was speaking to her. She nodded. "Yes, of course I'm okay." But the way she stood, the way her hands plucked at the skirt of her dress, the way her eyes darted all over the room nervously told a different story. He looked past her and noticed her wagon full of ugly dolls. What was going on with that? Maybe she was just playing a part for the Con, but a wagon of creepy dolls with disfigured faces?

He directed his attention back to Abby. "I know

it's a surprise to see me and all. We need to talk." He frowned again, noticing the way she clutched at the doll. He pressed gently. "Are you sure you're okay?"

"Yes," Abby said quickly, "I'm okay. Everything's fine." *Except that Patti hates you.* The doll trembled. Yes, Abby thought, she hates you very much.

They talked for a few minutes. It took some convincing, but Abby agreed to meet Jeremy later. Abby went to stand in front of the crowded elevators, carrying Patti and pulling her wagon of dolls. She wanted nothing more than to get into her room and be alone with her thoughts. After much jostling she managed to catch an elevator that had enough space for her and her wagon.

Minutes later she was in her room. She flung herself onto the bed and lay back against the pillows. She closed her eyes, trying to settle herself and calm herself enough to just relax and think peacefully. Even Patti remained silent for once. But Abby felt the doll's gaze boring holes into her psyche. Abby sighed and stared at the doll that had been such a pretty companion before the fire that had marred both their faces.

Abby ran her fingers across her own face, across the scars she still felt no matter how many times people told her they weren't there. How she longed for cool and beautiful skin, smooth like porcelain. Like the faces of her dolls. That's what her Abby doll was for. That's why she needed to find Crystal, the lady who told fortunes at the Con, the one who had introduced her to the forces of the Dark Arts and the magic of the Con. With all that she'd learned, combined with Patti's magic and the enchanting mystery of the Con, should allow Abby to achieve her wish. And when she got her wish, well, just maybe she would stop having the nightmares about the fire that had taken her family, destroyed her home and scarred her and her Patti doll for life.

Abby thought briefly back to the day when her mother had found the doll at a rummage sale and brought it home for her as a birthday present. The doll had enchanted her mother.

"I don't know what came over me, I just had to have her," Abby's mother said when she came home. "One minute I was telling the sales lady I wanted one of those, *My Friend and Me* dolls, and the next thing I knew, I found this little lady right here. She's a little old-timey looking, but I don't know what came over me. I thought I saw her in the clearance bin, but suddenly she was on the counter next to me. Hmm, there must have been two of them . . ."

Abby didn't care that Patti was an old-fashioned doll. She loved her on sight. It almost seemed that Patti had chosen, her, Abby, for a playmate. And lonely as she was with her older twin sisters always teasing her and being nasty, Abby had welcomed her new friend. Later, when she realized Patti had powers, she had kept it secret. It was their secret, theirs and theirs alone.

The next day Abby enjoyed the workshops. While she walked around people couldn't help staring in fascination of Abby's brood of broken dolls. And she, looking like a giant doll herself holding Patti, attracted many stares. People asked her to pose for pictures and Abby did so gladly. She didn't mind as long as she was disguised. And it was the Con. Strange looks were welcomed at the Con, encouraged even. That's why Abby loved the Con, anything could happen here, the mystery was almost magical. The Con was where even the deepest wishes could come true.

The day had been long and exciting, and finally it was time to meet Jeremy. They decided to have dinner at Sway, one of the Hyatt's more casual restaurants. To her own surprise and Jeremy's delight, Abby began to relax. She'd begun to think she and Jeremy had been the victims of some cosmic hoax. After the fire she'd been in the hospital, that Jeremy knew, but what had happened later?

"I called and called," Jeremy explained. "I came by, but nobody would let me see you."

"I was in a special ward," Abby said quietly.

Jeremy continued gently. "After that I was told you had moved away and I could never get anywhere. Then it was time to go off to college, and, I don't know, I guess I just sort of dropped the ball. I'm sorry."

"Water under the bridge," Abby said with a smile, but inwardly, way down inside, Abby finally admitted to herself what she had kept buried deep. Patti had been responsible for keeping them apart, the same way she had been responsible for causing the fire. Abby wondered what Jeremy would do when he saw her real face, her ugly scarred face, beneath the mask of the Con.

Despite her fears and worries, she accepted Jeremy's invitation to spend the next day together, laughing and talking, walking to the different hotels, trying to spot celebrities. They visited the vendor booths at the Mart. Jeremy bought a 'Star Wars' poster and a sword. Abby treated herself to a book about dark magic.

Jeremy wondered about her interest in the subject, but he was relieved to see least it wasn't a book about dolls. Still, he wondered what had happened to Abby. But they were having a nice time, like the old days, and Jeremy decided to ride the wave and just have fun. The only thing that disturbed him was the doll Abby continuously brought along with her. He couldn't help glancing at it time and time again, and he couldn't shake the feeling, no matter how ludicrous it was, that the doll hated him.

Jeremy's uneasy glances did not go unnoticed by Abby. They were having lunch at a restaurant near the hotel. She regarded him with solemn eyes and took a sip of her drink.

"Don't judge Patti too harshly," she said softly. "She was my friend when I had no one else."

She seemed so sad Jeremy let it go. He felt terrible that Abby didn't have anyone but a mutilated doll for a friend in her dark days, but that had been a long time ago. Jeremy just didn't like the doll. He never had, even before the fire when Abby would drag the dumb thing around with her. If he was going to rekindle his relationship with Abby it was going to be a twosome, not a threesome with some freaky, creepy doll constantly by her side.

Abby excused herself and went to the Ladies Room. For once she left the doll behind. Jeremy and the doll sat on opposite sides of their booth.

"Well, here we are," he said mockingly and toasted Patti.

The doll gazed off in the distance, turned a little to the side. Jeremy dropped his napkin and bent to retrieve it. When he sat up again it seemed something was different. It was the doll. She seemed to be sitting straighter and looking directly at him.

That's odd, Jeremy thought. But then maybe he had bumped the table when he picked up his napkin.

But wouldn't that make the doll slump and not sit straight up?

"Creepy little thing," Jeremy muttered. He turned away, looking for Abby. What was taking her so long? How long did he have to sit here with this thing?

Finally Abby came back and not a minute too soon. Jeremy was so relieved he didn't realize he'd been holding his breath. He glanced at the doll briefly, looked away and then looked back swiftly. For a second he thought he saw the doll's face change into a mask of hate. But the look was gone as quickly as it had come, and once again the doll with her cracked face and shattered eye stared ahead at nothing.

Jeremy decided to go back to the Mart. There were some other things he wanted to get. That was fine with her. Abby said that she wanted a break. They would meet later that night.

In her room, Abby rested. At the foot of her bed was her wagon of dolls. Next to her was her Abby doll. Abby was thinking about Crystal, the woman who told fortunes at the Con. She had been so swept up with Jeremy she had almost forgotten her mission.

She always avoided mirrors, but of course in her room there was a mirror in the alcove over the coffee maker and the large one in the bathroom. She never looked at her own reflection, but Jeremy made her forget her ugliness, and for a moment Abby contemplated taking off the makeup and taking her chances. She heard a loud sound in the bedroom and rushed out of the bathroom. Patti was on the bed, but the Abby doll was nowhere to be seen.

"What have you done!" Abby cried, but to her relief she found the Abby doll face down on the floor by the bed. There was a large bald spot where the doll's hair had been ripped out of her head. She found the clumps of doll hair on the bed next to Patti. The doll was mysteriously quiet.

"Don't touch her, do you understand?" She picked up the Abby doll and examined her closely. No real harm done. She had gotten there in time. But what about next time? She had to make the change before it was too late.

Late that afternoon Jeremy and Abby met for drinks and a light dinner at the 22 Stories Bar in the Atrium of the Hyatt Regency. Abby brought her creepy doll, Jeremy noticed, and part of him wished they were truly in a bar twenty-two stories high in a booth with a magnificent view, and he could pitch that damn doll from the window and get rid of it once and for all.

As soon as his mind voiced the thought, the doll seemed to shift in Abby's arms. For the barest moment Jeremy thought the glassy eyes lost their vacant stare and looked right at him. A chill passed through him.

"Are you cold?" Abby asked.

"Hmm? Uh, no, I'm not cold. Look, we have a table in the corner, by the window." He had bribed the hostess with a one-hundred-dollar-bill for that table, and he wasn't about to lose it.

"Wow," Abby exclaimed. "An actual table and by the window. I guess we got lucky."

"Yeah, we got real lucky," Jeremy said with a smile. "It's a shame it's on the ground floor," he muttered.

"Why? What do you mean?" Abby pulled her ugly doll closer to her side.

"Nothing," Jeremy said quickly. Her perception was uncanny. Or maybe it was her connection to the doll. "I just meant if we were higher up we'd have a better view."

Jeremy escorted Abby to the table. They ordered drinks and appetizers and sat back to relax. It had been a long day. The food came. Abby ate sparingly, but Jeremy was hungry. Even so, he found it hard to enjoy his food with that doll nestled next to Abby. He found himself drinking more than he normally would have, and by his third whiskey sour he had loosened up quite a bit.

"I love your costume, but I thought maybe you would have worn regular clothes for tonight. Or at least, not so much make-up." He frowned a little. "It's hard to see you under all that paint. It's like you're hiding away from the world."

Abby bit her lip and looked down at her plate.

Jeremy was immediately contrite. "I'm sorry. I shouldn't have said that."

"I would have thought at least you would understand," she murmured.

"What do you mean? Are you talking about the fire? That was a long time ago. I told you I tried to find you, but there was no trace of you."

"No, I don't mean that. I believe you." That was Patti, she thought.

"Then what?" Jeremy asked. He put one warm hand over Abby's cold one.

"I just don't want people staring at my face."

Jeremy stared at her with a bemused expression. "Why should people stare at your face? I mean you're pretty and all but—"

"I mean my scars, Jeremy, my scars! Don't pretend with me, not you." She began to cry softly.

"Abby, don't cry," Jeremy said. A dark thought

occurred to him. He was beginning to understand.

"Abby," he told her firmly. "I don't know what you see when you look in the mirror, but you're not scarred or disfigured in any way." He glanced at the doll.

"Oh, come on," Abby sniffed. "Come to think of it, maybe you just feel sorry for me. Is that why we're here? Because you don't have to pity me." She looked down at her hands. "And soon it will be different," she said in a low whisper. "If you can just wait a little longer."

"What do you mean? Never mind, it doesn't matter." He leaned forward. "I'm telling you, I don't see any scars." At least not on the outside, he thought. Immediately he felt bad for his unkind thought. "You really do see scars, don't you?" He surprised himself by adding, "Is that what she told you?" He indicated the doll, shocking himself and Abby, but before Abby could respond Jeremy raised his glass to take a drink of his fourth whiskey sour. He glanced at the doll with her cracked face and broken eye. "I mean, your doll there, she's messed up, but you—"

The glass in his hand shattered.

Jeremy cried out as a shard cut his lip. Abby screamed. "What the hell!" What hadn't cut his lip had exploded all over the table.

Abby became upset. "I'm sorry, Jeremy, really I am. Really, Jeremy, it's all my fault."

"What are you talking about?" Jeremy asked as their server ran over to help.

"I'm so sorry, sir, are you all right?" He noticed Jeremy's bleeding lip. "Would you like to see a doctor? Let me get the manager."

Jeremy blotted his lip with napkin. "I'm fine,

really, thank you. I don't need anything, really."

While Jeremy and the server spoke Abby glared down at the doll. The exchange wasn't meant for his eyes, but he saw it, and he wondered again just what was wrong with Abby. Whatever it was, it was because of that doll, and suddenly he knew he couldn't have one without the other.

Their evening ended awkwardly after the glass shattered in Jeremy's hand. Jeremy waved away Abby's offers to doctor him and said he'd see her later.

Abby noted Jeremy's swift departure. "You shouldn't have done that," Abby said to her doll.

"What?" the server asked, looking at Abby curiously.

Abby was familiar with that look. It was time to take Patti and leave.

"Nothing," Abby said quickly. "I was just talking to myself." She tossed a hefty tip on the table and left the bar.

Abby was lost in her thoughts when she entered the elevator. She was upset that Patti hated Jeremy and tried to hurt him. And what he said about her not having any scars, could it have been true? No, she thought he was just being kind. What was she going to do? She had to find Crystal, the woman who told fortunes at Con.

Abby had always watched others having their fortunes told by the woman who called herself Crystal. She always lingered close by, watching, but never had the courage to ask. Finally, last year, after having finished up with several people, Crystal turned to Abby.

"Would you like to have your fortune told?"

Abby felt nervous but she nodded.

"Well, come on then," the fortune teller said

amiably and shuffled her deck of tarot cards.

They sat at the corner of Crystal's small table in the corner of the hallway. Crystal laid out the cards and considered them. She frowned as if perplexed, then mumbling under breath, swiped the cards back into her hands, shuffled them, and dealt again.

Once more she stared at the cards, staring at them for so long Abby thought the woman she was lost in a daydream. Then the fortune teller mumbled something under her breath and looked at Abby. She stared so deeply that Abby was sure she could see through her painted clown face and see her scars.

Finally, she spoke.

"Beauty lies in the eyes of the beholder," she said, and before Abby could roll her eyes at the cliché she'd heard a thousand times before, the woman added softly, "be careful what you wish for." Then she packed up her cards and left. Abby hadn't seen her since.

Be careful what you wish for . . .

In the last year Abby had thought of that message a hundred times.

The elevator doors closed. Abby's thoughts were still on Jeremy, so it took a moment for her to feel the shift in the air around her. The elevator lights seemed to dim and fade. She heard the drone of chatter. The bubble that had cocooned her thoughts popped. She surfaced to what was real around her and was surprised to find herself alone with the exception to one other person who chatted amiably.

Abby wondered who the woman was speaking to. She looked closer, surprised the woman was actually Crystal, the very person she had wanted to find. But what was she saying? She was chattering away at full speed, spewing nonsense, it seemed.

"Did you hear me?" Crystal had turned to face Abby. Suddenly Abby wasn't so sure it was her.

"Crystal?"

The woman stared at Abby.

"Isn't your name Crystal?"

The woman's mouth opened and she began to speak, but there was something about her that was odd and frightening and coldly distant.

"Oh, Crystal shmistal," the woman said and then she tilted her head back stiffly and laughed.

Her laughter stopped as suddenly as it started. Crystal turned to stare at Abby. Her head and neck and shoulders moved in one unit. She reminded Abby of a robot, and there was something bizarre about that stare that made her think of Patti. She clutched the doll tightly. Crystal's eyes held a strange look. The light dimmed. A reddish haze seemed to fill the small space of the elevator.

Abby gasped, looking around, suddenly realizing with surprise, that at this crowded conference, there were only the two of them in the elevator. Sometimes it took twenty minutes to get an elevator, and even then you had to squeeze in.

The woman was speaking again.

"Excuse me?" Abby asked, backing away from her as far as she could.

"I said, wishes do come true," the woman said in a jovial voice. "What do you wish for, Abby?" The lights dimmed. Crystal's voice dropped an octave lower to a buzzing drone. *"What do you wish forrr . . . ?"*

Suddenly there was no light in the elevator. All the air seemed to rush out like a vacuum. Abby pulled back in fear. Crystal's eyes glowed red in the darkness.

"Be careful what you wish for . . ." the woman droned, then she grinned, making the reddish glow in her eyes all the more terrible and wicked.

Abby shrieked and latched onto Patti. But the doll seemed so stiff and unyielding, so full of . . . malice. Abby looked down. The doll's eyes glowed red also, twin embers of a demon's eyes.

"*Be careful what you wish for,*" the doll mimicked, and then cackled with maniacal laughter.

Abby dropped Patti and screamed and screamed.

"I just wanted to be beautiful, I just wanted Jeremy to love me," she tried to cry out, but Patti read her thoughts.

"*He'll love you forever and ever, never fear, Abby dearest,*" the doll chirped. Her red eyes glowed feverishly. "*Forever and ever . . .*"

Patti's evil laughter joined Crystal's and grew louder and louder until Abby could do nothing but scream until she fainted in the dark.

Abby awoke in her room. Consumed by the vision of red eyes and crazy laughter, she opened her mouth to scream before she realized she was no longer in the dark elevator. She was safe on the bed in her room. Patti lay next to her. To Abby's relief, everything had returned to normal. She had just suffered from a terrible nightmare.

"Oh, Patti, thank goodness you're okay," she told her, relieved the doll was back to normal. The memory of the elevator will still too upsetting. "I think I'll go take a hot bath." She paused. "You know, Patti, I was just thinking about what Jeremy said. Maybe I should go back and see those doctors. The ones you said were no good."

"They lie," the doll murmured, *"and he lies, too. They all lie. I'm the only one who loves you, Abby. Just me. Don't you remember, Abby, don't you? I tried to pull you back from the fire, didn't I? That's how I got hurt, saving you. And now you want to leave meeeee."*

She stared at Abby, capturing her within her lifeless gaze. Abby felt rooted to that stare. "No, Patti," she said dully. "I don't want to leave you, not ever."

"Nobody loved me, Abby, they all hated me, your mean sisters hated me, even your precious mother and Jeremy."

Abby found herself nodding.

"You don't need him, dearest Abby, you just need me. Just you and me. Forever. He thinks you're ugly," Patti said meanly. *"He laughs at you. He wants to leave you, too. And he lies."*

Patti's cruel words brought tears to Abby's eyes, but Patti's last comment jerked Abby back to her senses. Jeremy may have forgotten about her, he may have gone on to live his own life, but Jeremy had had never lied to her.

Abby needed to think clearly. With all her strength, she tore herself away from Patti's horrible stare.

The air around his bristled with Patti's rage.

"No, Patti, leave me alone, I want to think. I'm going to take a long, quiet bath now. I'm tired."

The Abby doll lay behind a pillow. Abby didn't see it.

She pulled off her wig, grabbed her robe and headed for the bathroom. She missed Patti's sneer, but the doll's whisper trailed after.

"Yesss, Abby dearest, I'll leave you alone now. To cleanse and purify your soul."

Abby barely heard her as she closed the door to the bathroom. Her thoughts full of her lost love, Abby had forgotten about her new Abby doll stuffed behind a pillow, left alone with Patti. She turned on the faucets and filled the tub. Soon she was immersed in warm water, to purge and cleanse away the sins of the day.

When Abby stepped out of the tub at least an hour later, she felt calmer and more relaxed. Her thoughts had been consumed by her feelings for Jeremy. To her surprise, she hadn't even thought of her dolls. Feeling braver than usual, she had even washed off all her makeup.

She couldn't summon up the courage to look in the mirror, but when she touched her face the thick feel of her scars had faded.

Maybe she *was* getting better. Maybe she didn't need the dark arts and black magic. Maybe the lies weren't coming from Jeremy. And after what had happened in the elevator, she didn't want to seek out Crystal anymore. She couldn't forget the woman's glowing eyes and evil laughter, even if it only had been a nightmare. Most importantly, she couldn't wait to talk to Jeremy. Perhaps fate had reunited them here, at the Con, for a reason. Maybe it was her last chance for happiness.

Abby emerged from the bathroom, pulled the belt of her robe tight around her waist and stopped in her tracks.

Patti's shrill voice greeted her. *"I've been waiting for you, Abby dearest."*

"No!" Abby whispered. Before her was her worst nightmare come true.

She had forgotten about her Abby doll, had left it unprotected and Patti had seized the moment. The doll seemed unharmed but was locked within Patti's clutches. They were both seated on the cushioned chair by the window. Somehow Patti had procured a knife.

"Compliments of room service, dearest Abby." The doll giggled.

On the table by chair, her book of the Dark Arts lay open. Patti had been reading it. While she enjoyed a warm relaxing bath, Patti had been very busy, indeed.

The blood drained from her face as Abby took everything in. She had let down her guard. That had been her big mistake, to let herself love again.

"Patti," Abby began slowly. "don't."

The doll's voice rose. *"You were planning to leave me, dearest Abby."*

"Patti, stop, you have to be careful."

"You wished for beauty for yourself but would leave me ugly and alone. You would leave me for him."

Air stirred in the room, strengthened to a gale by Patti's fury. Impossible, but anything was possible when you mixed evil with the magic of the Con. Anything at all.

"I was going to have your face fixed, Patti, I told you many times, but you wouldn't let me."

"Because you would have sent me away," Patti screeched. *"And now you'll have your precious wish. You can be a beautiful doll!"*

Patti lifted the knife.

"No!" Abby screamed. "Noooooo!"

The pages of the book fluttered to a special passage. The doll's voice rose, more terrible because of its childish timbre. *"I offer this sacrifice, O father of Darkness,"*

With a swift movement Patti lifted her

porcelain arm and stabbed the Abby doll. The doll emitted a tiny sound, but Abby flinched and screamed. She grabbed her side. Her hands came back bloody.

"Stop!" Abby sobbed, bent over with pain, "Please stop."

The childish voice continued in a droning voice, high pitched and evil.

"The flesh of this spirit shall reek with decay,"

Patti stabbed the doll again. Abby screamed and crumpled to the floor, bleeding from wounds wielded by her crazed doll and black magic.

"Rich and ripe, I offer this daughter,
O Master of darkness, I give unto thee."

The knife raised again.

Abby tried one last time, "Patti, please," she begged. "Please."

But the knife lowered, stabbing again and again. Abby screamed and wailed, writhing on the floor, her hands clawing and beating against an unseen assailant.

"Be careful what you wish for, dearest Abby." The doll screamed. *"Did you think I would let you leave me for him?"* The knife raised and lowered. *"Don't worry, dearest Abby, we'll all be together soon, forever. . ."*

"What have I done?" Abby murmured with her last breath. "Not him! Oh, Jeremy, I'm so sorry."

Hearing Jeremy's name, the vengeful doll shrieked in rage. She struck Abby doll's head over and over until it lay smashed and broken. Then, with her smalls arms outstretched, her white fingers curled into claws. She flew at Abby on wings of evil and fastened to her.

"Be careful what you wish for, dearest Abby!"

she screamed over and over.

But Abby no longer heard her. Her head was gone.

***

Jeremy was in his room, contemplating the evening's events. He was beyond wondering about Abby. He just wanted to wish her and her doll well and be on his way, but his conscience pricked at him and sleep eluded him. Was it right to turn his back on her? He didn't really want to forget about her. It was that doll. If he could get Abby away from that doll she could enjoy some happiness in her life, he was sure of it.

His laptop blipped. He looked at the desk table. That was odd, maybe he'd received some kind of hotel message. The screen glowed eerily. Jeremy got out of the bed and went to the desk. He turned the monitor towards himself and tapped the enter key. The face of Abby's terrible doll floated up from hell and stared at him through the computer screen.

Jeremy jumped back a foot. "Holy Jesus!" he cried out in fear.

The doll stared at him for a long moment, her glassy black eyes fathomless. She began to speak. Jeremy's eyes widened in disbelief. Her voice was very high and piercing. It made him think of sour lemons.

"*Hello, Jeremy,*" she piped in her high doll voice. "*Would you like to play?*"

Jeremy stared in fascinated horror. How was this happening? His hands felt frozen. He looked down at them. They were shaking.

"*No?*" the doll asked brightly. "*I didn't think so. Poor Abby. She'll miss you. She wanted to be beautiful. That's all she wanted. That's what she wished for.*" The doll cocked her head to one side and winked at him. *"If you change your mind we'll be in room 813."* A piece of glass around her shattered eye fell away, it was black beneath.

Jeremy gasped. He thought he would vomit.

"Oh well," the Patti doll squeaked. *"Time to go. It wouldn't do to fall to pieces."* She tilted her head back and laughed, *"Ha Ha Ha!"*

The black maw of the mouth widened. The black void filled the screen then blipped out completely. Without the light of the monitor the room was cast in complete darkness.

Jeremy's heart filled with dread. His first instinct was to flee the hotel and never look back. Then he thought of Abby. She must be in trouble. That doll had gotten stronger, if such a thing was possible. What had happened?

"Oh no, Abby!" he cried. "What have you done?" He rushed out of his room.

Jeremy raced to Abby's room. He banged on the door loudly, shouting her name. Nothing.

"Abby!"

He pounded again and wrestled the handle of the door. Locked. He looked down. The color over the key swipe magically changed color. Instead of red, indicating the door was locked, the color popped to green, as if to welcome him in. The hair stood up at the back of Jeremy's neck. He placed his hand on the lever. This time it turned in his hand easily. *Click.*

Pushing the door open, he was immediately assailed by a cloud of smoke and dust and began coughing. Beneath the fog was an unpleasant smell, but as soon as he entered the room the hazy mess took on a lengthening shape and curled away, disappearing through the vents as if summoned away by a snake charmer. The bad smell, however, remained.

Jeremy fanned the air in front of his face with his hand, but the last cough dried in his throat like ashes, for as the cloud of dusky smog wafted away, revealed before Jeremy's eyes was a scene from his most fervent of nightmares, as bad as the doll's face talking to him from his computer screen.

On the bed lay a life sized doll. It wore a floral lace dress and the hair cascaded across the pillows in perfect ringlets. Then Jeremy realized this was no doll, but a human body, Abby's body. Even with the different hair and the old fashioned dress, he knew her.

"Abby!" he exclaimed, but his voice emerged rough and hoarse. He stared at the body lying limp and lonely on the hotel bed. He half expected to see her hands clasped around a bouquet of flowers, like a corpse in a casket, but one hand, the right one, dangled from the bed. For a horrible moment he thought the hand would reach up, twisting and rising before reaching out to grab him.

If you be a dead thing, please don't move, his mind whimpered.

He had a sense of being watched. The silence was deafening, the air around him stifling. Still he could not bring himself to move. A feeling of dread grew inside him and gnawed. He was on the very precipice of something.

Again, that feeling of being watched by eyes hidden somewhere in this room. His dread grew wings and unfurled into terror. He glanced at the wagon of Abby's ugly dolls at the foot of the bed. They stared back at him. Jeremy shuddered. He didn't like all those dolls. They stared at nothing with those gaping eyes, but when you looked away . . .

But then, in the murky stillness of the room. Jeremy heard a sound, a furtive sound, as faint as a soft wind sighing through the trees on a cold autumn night. The sound was so delicately slight, so tiny in this infinitesimal moment, but nevertheless it caught his attention as Jeremy knew it was meant to do.

Jeremy dragged his gaze away from the wagon of dolls and saw Abby's Patti doll sitting in a chair beneath the window. The night cast a shadow across the doll's face, but a sliver of light from a sickly yellow moon beam illuminated part of the doll's ravaged features. She sat in the shadows mostly, but Jeremy caught a glint of malice, a burning hatred meant for him, or perhaps this doll was the embodiment of malevolent evil. The rustle of fabric against the chair made him shiver. The doll had moved on its own.

Jeremy's heart juddered in his chest. An icy cold finger of fear slipped down his spine. The hair stood up on the back of his neck, for he noticed that beneath the white porcelain hand lying demurely in her lap was an object. It caught the glare of the moon and glimmered. It was a knife perhaps, but slick with something sick and shiny. It came to him from the darkness.

"Hello Jeremy, how nice of you to come." That horrible voice again.

"You and Abby have been very bad. You were going to take her away from me, but I have a surprise for you."

Jeremy's mind screamed, *"RUN!"* He wanted nothing more than to open the door, tear out of that room and never look back, but he couldn't move. His feet felt like they were weighed down by cement blocks

The heaviness in the room seemed to lift

slightly. Jeremy realized that the lights were actually on, it was just an ominous cloud of doom that made the room seem so dark and dimly lit. Or maybe it was just that creepy doll, sitting beneath the window, with the flicker of yellow moonlight glinting in her glass eye talking to him. Maybe that was the reason.

. . .*yea, though I walk through the valley of the shadow of death, I will fear no evil . . .*

The passage floated through his brain and he forced himself to look away from the doll. Even through his fear he looked sadly at Abby. The doll had stolen Abby's emaciated soul once and for all.

"Poor Abby," Jeremy said softly. "What have you done?"

But even through his sorrow Jeremy detected something amiss. It took him a moment before he realized what was wrong.

The body of Abby now had the head of a doll.

"Do you like your surprise?" The doll giggled. The sound was like nails screeching against a chalk board.

But this time Jeremy's amazement overrode his terror. He peered closer. It couldn't be. "Abby?" He moved a step closer, his eyes taking in the obscenity before him. The head was giant sized in proportion to the body, but with skin that was smooth, porcelain perfect and unscarred. Jeremy reached out a tentative hand, but he couldn't quite bring himself to touch it. His unsure hand hovered. The skin was flawless. Yet at the same time it was . . .

Unholy his mind whispered.

It was like someone had spoken the word right inside his brain, jolting him like a splash of icy water, and he snatched his hand back quickly.

Before his horrified gaze, the doll's hinged eyes suddenly snapped open. They stared straight up at the ceiling. Jeremy's mouth went dry. Then slowly the head, as if detached from the body, shifted and began turning, as if the Abby-thing wanted to look at Jeremy but couldn't control her mechanical movements. The head finally landed at an oddly grotesque angle, as if the eyes would stare into the pillow. The effect was unnatural, a feat no human body could perform.

Her glassy eyes searched and trained on Jeremy. For the barest moment, the expression in the doll's eyes was one of sorrow before it drifted away, the last vestige of her lost humanity seeping away through her cold porcelain pores. She had become a doll, complete and grotesque with flawless skin and rosy cheeks.

As if pulled by an unseen hand, the head and torso of the doll seem to lift on its own, slowly upward, like an eerie magic trick. As it sat up the large head remained cocked at Jeremy while the body faced the other direction. Jeremy thought the head would pop off and roll to the floor. But the head remained glued, perpendicular to the body. The effect was grotesque. He backed away slowly, yet he couldn't tear his eyes away.

Unholy! the voice inside Jeremy screamed again.

The body began to twist around to align itself with the head. It emitted a stiff and creaky sound, the opening of a crypt from the grave. Her shiny patent leather shoes dangled from beneath the torn hem of the dress. The body finally stopped, having arranged itself beneath the doll's head, so that now the entire body faced him.

The painted features began to contort and writhe against the white porcelain face. Jeremy's breath came out in a gasp. It was trying to smile. The pink mouth twitched and turned up at the corners, but what emerged was a leer, a stretching of features that were incapable of human emotion. And the eyes! Dead and soulless, but at the same time gleefully rich with churning evil. Jeremy's blood turned even colder. The fear rose and crouched within Jeremy, so great a fear even his testicles shriveled up in cowardice and tried to crawl back into the safe warm flesh of his body.

The eyes stared relentlessly. Again the invisible hand pulled. The right hand, the one that had dangled from the bed, raised stiffly. She was reaching for him, Jeremy realized. The bile rose in his throat, if that thing touched him . . .

"No," he croaked. He backed away until he bumped into the wall behind him.

The doll opened its rosy pink mouth. *"Jeremeeeeeeee."*

Jeremy's skin broke out in goosebumps. His body poured sweat, but it was cold and clammy against his skin. It was calling him.

"Jeremeeeeeeee," it seemed to wail and then tapered off.

Suddenly it cried out in a shrill voice, *"Look what I can do!"*

The head was turning again but this time rotating slowly like a pig on a spit, until it twisted completely around in a 360 degree circle. Jeremy realized with sick clarity that this was her way of preening and doing a pirouette. A head doing a pirouette without the body. Jeremy tried to swallow, but he couldn't. The Abby thing was trying to flirt. Just the head, because the body was dead. The head stopped turning. The pink lips twisted and pulled.

"*Be careful what you wish for!*" the doll suddenly shrieked in a squeaky inhuman voice. "*Aren't I beautiful?*"

Was *this* what Abby had wanted? No, Jeremy knew it wasn't, but her mind had been warped by that doll and it had tricked her. But through it all, Abby now had what mattered most to her. She had achieved her wish. She had perfect, flawless skin. The scars were gone, at least on the surface.

"*Aren't I beautiful?*" the doll shrieked again, and this time tears flowed from the gaping eyes. Ah, such anguish! It would have been heart breaking if it hadn't been so ghastly. Abby was trapped inside the dead thing. He wanted to get her out, yet he wanted to run screaming from the room just as badly.

"*Be careful what you wish for! Be careful what you wish for!*" the doll screamed over and over. A warning? Regret? Then suddenly the tears dried up, vanished. Abby was gone. The doll had stolen Abby's emaciated soul once and for all.

From its perch beneath the window, the Patti doll cocked its head and giggled. Her laughing mouth revealed milk white teeth, but even those little teeth seemed sinister, like daggers against the doll's face.

Behind him he heard the door to the room slam shut. Ah, yes, the magic of Magna Con, where anything can happen.

The Abby doll reached out again. Jeremy recoiled.

"*Jeremeeee,*" the Abby thing squeaked in its doll voice, reaching.

"No! Stay away!" Jeremy tried to run, but he

was paralyzed by fear. The large head jostled loosely like a door swinging on a broken hinge. For all her porcelain beauty, she was hideous.

"Be careful what you wish for!"

Jeremy watched as the life-size Abby doll slowly moved to rise. The shiny patent leather doll shoes landed on the floor with a thump. With her first thick step the strap of one shiny shoe snapped, but undeterred, the doll took a lurched towards Jeremy, its mechanical gait as unsteady and unsure as a baby taking its first steps, reaching for the loving arms of its mother. The large head rocked from side to side, bobbing and bouncing.

"Be careful what you wish for! I'm so beautiful!" the Abby doll shrieked, jerking forward.

Jeremy screamed and tried to escape, but the door knob rattled uselessly. He was trapped in the room with no way out, for Magna Con had its powers, and Abby had paid a heavy price. He was part of the deal, he realized, when she'd sold her soul to that evil doll.

There were some things worse than scars, he thought crazily. Much worse. Maybe that pinkish mouth soon would be turning red. Jeremy heard the giggle of the Patti doll. Her giggle became louder and louder until it was an evil cackle reverberating over and over in his brain. Jeremy screamed as the doll descended.

"Abby! No!" Jeremy screamed over and over. "Abby!"

Through it all, Jeremy could hear Abby's Patti doll's high pitched laughter. Jeremy screamed and screamed and then he screamed some more. She descended on him.

"Kiss meeeeee . . ."
It became unspeakable.

***

The next morning dawned bright and sunny. It was a clear crisp day, cooler than usual for this time of year. The frenzy of Magna Con, having peaked, would be winding down. The cleaning ladies made their rounds, going from room to room.

At room 813 Mary Bishop, a cleaning woman at the hotel for four years, knocked on the door.

"Housekeeping!" she called.

No one answered. She knocked again. Finally, she used her key and entered the room. Broken shards of glass or some kind of porcelain lay strewn about the carpet. She looked around in surprise. There was a red wagon at the foot of the bed, but it was empty. Then she saw the dolls on the bed. A boy and a girl. They lay side by side, like a couple. What nice dolls, she thought. The girl doll had a smile, but the boy doll did not. She examined closer and noticed the girl doll had the boy doll's wrist clutched in one hand. Mary Bishop looked at the faces, the girl doll's mouth seemed to smile and give her a sly wink.

Mary's eyes widened. "Mother of God!" she whispered fearfully. She opened the door and ran into the hall.

In the room directly across the hall another cleaning woman was hard at work changing sheets and grumbling under her breath. The door to the room she cleaned was propped open. She heard her name being shouted from the hallway.

"Lizzie!"

They met at the doorway. "What's up with you,

Mary? Stop goofin' around." Lizzie took in her friend's pallor. Mary was clutching the supply cart weakly. "You okay?" Lizzie peered past Mary and looked into the room. "What's going in there, you find a dead body or somethin'?"

"It's nothing," Mary said. "Just some dolls on the bed. I guess they just kind of freaked me out a little."

"What are you talking about? Here, have some water and sit down in there."

She indicated the room she was cleaning, took a bottle of water from the supply cart, opened it and handed it to Mary. Waving away Mary's thanks, Lizzie went into room 813 and immediately spotted two dolls on the bed.

"Well, look at this," Lizzie said. She emerged from the room bringing them with her. "Someone left these dolls behind. Look how pretty they are."

Mary grimaced. "I don't like them, just take them to the Lost and Found."

"Huh, no way, finders keepers, losers weepers." She wrapped the dolls in a towel and set them in her cart. "These two are coming home with me. My grandbaby's turning seven this weekend and she just loves dolls. And these two are already in love."

Mary glanced at the dolls reluctantly. There was something about the boy doll's eyes. She couldn't help but feel a sense of anguish. And that girl doll. It had perfect skin, smooth and flawless, but if you looked closely . . . Mary crossed herself. If Lizzie wanted those dolls she could have them. She didn't want to go back in that room.

"Hey, Lizzie," Mary said suddenly, "do me a favor and trade rooms with me."

"Are you kiddin', I'm already half way through here."

"I'll take an extra room for you," Mary told her. "You can take extra time for lunch."

Lizzie shrugged. "All right, that's okay by me. Just don't mess with my new dolls."

Mary looked away. "Don't worry, I won't touch them."

"You know," Lizzie said. "I think I'll take these two with me in here." She picked up the dolls carefully. "You come with grandma," she said. "My little Sherry is going to be so excited when she sees you. She's kind of shy, but she sure loves dolls, just loves 'em."

The boy doll with the sad eyes stared straight ahead. Not the girl doll. She grinned craftily, but Lizzie didn't notice.

Yet.

She entered room 813 carrying the dolls. "This was her lucky day."

About Yasmin Bakhtiari

Yasmin lives in Atlanta, Georgia with her family. She enjoys Zumba, cooking, reading, yoga and swimming. Yasmin has been a member of Georgia Romance Writers and Romance Writers of America for years and enjoys meeting and writing with her critique partners.

Yasmin's latest adventure is the production of the movie Evil Little Things based upon her original stories published by Gilded Dragonfly Books.

Connect with Yasmin

https://www.facebook.com/profile.php?id=10
0008131757148

Contact Yasmin

yasmimbakhtiari40@gmail.com